Terrible Tiger

M. Faksimily

ILLUSTRATED BY
ROBERT BROOMFIELD

Mister Faksimily and the TIGER

ANITA HEWETT

FOLLETT PUBLISHING COMPANY

CHICAGO   NEW YORK

Text copyright © 1967 by Anita Hewett.
Illustrations copyright © 1967 by The Bodley Head, Ltd.
First published 1967 by The Bodley Head, Ltd., London.

Published 1969 in the United States of America by Follett Publishing Company, Chicago.

Library of Congress Catalog Card Number: 69-10253

First Printing

T/L 6022

Terrible Tiger lived in the jungle.
He was huge and ferocious.
He hated photographers.
He *ate* photographers, cameras and all.

Mr. Faksimily went to the jungle with his camera,
his umbrella, and a clean white handkerchief.
The jungle was hot and wild and rampageous.

"Oh dear me!" said Mr. Faksimily.
Then he set off through the great green
trees. In the branches above there were
little brown monkeys. They stared with
their shining black eyes, and they said:
"Where are you going, funny little fat man?
What are you doing in our hot wild jungle?"
"I'm going to take a photograph
of Terrible Tiger."
"No you aren't. We won't let you pass.
We won't let you pass through our
great green trees."

The monkeys took nuts in their skinny brown paws and flung them down on Mr. Faksimily. Mr. Faksimily opened his umbrella, and the nuts bounced off it into the undergrowth. Except for seven extra hard little nuts, which made seven little holes in the big black umbrella. So Mr. Faksimily got through the trees.

On through the jungle went Mr. Faksimily, until he came to a
turbid brown river. On the bank of the river stood a maribou
stork. It stood on its scraggy long legs, and it said:
"Where are you going, funny little fat man?
What are you doing in my hot wild jungle?"
"I'm going to take a photograph
of Terrible Tiger."
"No you aren't. You can't cross
my river. How will you know
where the deep water lies?"

Mr. Faksimily took off his boots and slung them
over his shoulders by the laces. He took his
umbrella and prodded the river bed.
Where the water was deep, it came to the handle.
Where the water was shallow, it covered the spike.
Mr. Faksimily walked in safe water.
So he got across the river to the opposite bank.

On the opposite bank was a mango tree,
with a great mottled python snake
twisted around a branch. The python snake
flickered its tongue, and it said:
"Where are you going, funny little fat man?
What are you doing in my hot wild jungle?"
"I'm going to take a photograph
of Terrible Tiger."
"No you aren't. You can't
pass my mango tree. How
can you walk with wet socks
on your feet?"

Mr. Faksimily opened his umbrella. He took
off his socks and wrung them out and hung
them to dry on the big black umbrella.
So Mr. Faksimily got past the mango tree.

On through the jungle went Mr. Faksimily, until he came to a bamboo thicket. In the bamboo thicket stood an arrogant peacock. It lifted its arrogant beak, and it said:

"Where are you going, funny little fat man? What are you doing in my hot wild jungle?"

"I'm going to take a photograph of Terrible Tiger."

"No you aren't. You can't pass my thicket. I'll frighten you so that you'll turn your back."

The arrogant peacock spread out its feathers, and scores of inquisitive feathery eyes seemed to be staring at Mr. Faksimily.

"I can do that," said Mr. Faksimily.

He opened his umbrella, and the seven little holes were seven little eyes, staring at the peacock. The arrogant peacock closed its feathers and turned its back on Mr. Faksimily. So Mr. Faksimily got through the thicket.

On through the jungle went Mr. Faksimily, until he came
to a muddy black swamp. In the middle of the swamp
stood a huffy rhinoceros. It shuffled its feet in the mud,
and it said:

"Where are you going, funny little fat man? What are
you doing in my hot wild jungle?"

"I'm going to take a photograph of Terrible Tiger."

"No you aren't. You can't pass my swamp. I shall toss
you into the air on my horn."

Mr. Faksimily took his umbrella and pointed its spike
at the huffy rhinoceros. "Bang bang bang bang bang!"
he shouted. The huffy rhinoceros was rather shortsighted.
He thought that the big black umbrella was a gun, and
he stayed where he was in the middle of the mud.

So Mr. Faksimily got past the swamp.

On through the jungle went Mr. Faksimily, until
he came to a grassy clearing. In the clearing there was
one tall tree and an elephant. The elephant curled
up its trunk, and it said:
"Where are you going, funny little fat man?
What are you doing in my hot wild jungle?"
"I'm going to take a photograph of Terrible Tiger."
"No you aren't. You can't pass my clearing.
I'll stamp you into the ground with my feet."
Mr. Faksimily took his umbrella and hooked
its handle over a branch. Then he pulled
himself up, hook and heave, hook and heave,
up to the middle of the very tall tree.

Mr. Faksimily sat in the tree, and presently,
distantly, faintly at first, he heard something growling.
Far below, at the edge of the clearing, an angry striped
face with whiskers appeared.

"Terrible Tiger," called Mr. Faksimily. "Here I am,
in your hot wild jungle, waiting to take a photograph
of you. But you look so small, being so far away.
Won't you come closer, Terrible Tiger?"

Terrible Tiger growled again.

"Funny little fat man, put away your gun."

"It isn't a gun," said Mr. Faksimily.

Then Mr. Faksimily took his umbrella and tied his white
handkerchief on to the spike. Terrible Tiger saw the white flag,
and he came a little closer, and yet a little closer, until he was
sitting near the bottom of the tree. He still looked small, being
so far below, but his growl sounded fiercer and more ferocious.

"Funny little fat man, good to eat, here
I shall sit until you come down."
"Oh dear me!" said Mr. Faksimily. "Then if
you'll allow me, I'll take your photograph."
Mr. Faksimily hung his umbrella carefully
over a nearby branch. Then he focused his
camera on Terrible Tiger.
"Smile at the camera please, Mr. Tiger."

While Mr. Faksimily was talking to the tiger,
a colony of ants came swarming up the tree.
They settled on the big black umbrella and
ate it. All that they left behind was the skeleton.
Mr. Faksimily didn't notice.
"Smile," he said. "Smile, Mr. Tiger."

It was hot in the middle of the very tall tree. Mr. Faksimily took
his umbrella and held it over his head for a sunshade. Terrible
Tiger stopped his growling and stared very hard at the skeleton
umbrella.

"Oh dear me!" said Mr. Faksimily. "My umbrella isn't keeping
off the sun. I wonder why?"

Terrible Tiger started to smile.

"How very, very sad!" said Mr. Faksimily. "Somebody has
eaten my best umbrella."

Then Terrible Tiger started to laugh.
He rolled on his back with his paws in
the air. He laughed himself helpless.
Mr. Faksimily held the camera steady
and took a careful photograph
of Terrible Tiger.

"That's *that* job done," said Mr. Faksimily, and he hooked
himself down from the very tall tree. He only stopped once on
his way through the jungle, to talk to a friendly fat parrot in a bush.
And then he went home, and the parrot went with him,
in a cage made neatly from the skeleton umbrella.
So Mr. Faksimily got home safely.
"It's a pity my umbrella was eaten," he said. "But I really
mustn't grumble. It was useful to the end."

Terrible Tiger

M. Faksimily